STABLE GOSSIP

JOANNA FISHER

Copyright © Joanna Fisher 2016
Illustrations © Eric Heyman 2016

Stable Gossip® is the registered trademark
of Joanna Fisher.

Published by
Candy Jar Books
Mackintosh House
136 Newport Road, Cardiff, CF24 1DJ
www.candyjarbooks.co.uk

ISBN: 978-0-9935192-6-0

Edited by Will Rees, Shaun Russell, Tamsin Hackett,
& Lauren Thomas
Cover by Will Brooks & Eric Heyman

Dedicated to:

Elizabeth
Wheldon
Zelda
Jack
Kinsey

And my Mum & Dad

As the Fantasy and Mystery of words capture our minds, the beauty and enchantment of Horses capture our Hearts.

Knowing their souls gallop over land and jump over valleys, their elegance and grace live on forever.

In Loving Memory of:

Coco

Flo

Nosey

Rumbo

Charmeur

Leo

The wonderful world of horses is a place where adults and children share their passion, dedication and devotion to an animal who knows no malice, is submissive, loyal and equally intelligent.

Where a partnership of trust and hard work pays off and the feeling of love congregates in shared hearts. Any Horse lover would agree!

The 'magical' world of horses, however, stems deeper, beneath what one hears, further than one sees and yet becomes as clear as day to those blessed with the ability to look beyond. For horses talk, horses feel, horses want, horses think and never, ever forget.

I will now share with you a little magic, allowing my readers a glimpse of what really goes on in their world, so aptly named… *Stable Gossip*.

These are true stories from my own horses. They brought me the happiest memories!

Nosey

Nosey is an opinionated chestnut dressage horse in training. It is nearly impossible to distract him from his busy schedule.

Rumbo

A very big black dressage youngster,
eager to learn and grow.

Flo

Flo's mother was a dressage princess, and Flo is very proud of the fact that this makes her a princess too. Prim and proper, she wishes all the other horses would just behave.

Coco

A true dressage diva of Olympic magnitude; a beauty in dark brown, patient, polite, correct –
simply perfect in every way.

Charmeur

A grey top show jumper, Charmeur has been there, seen it and done it, and has the Rosettes to prove it!

Leo

An unflappable grey show jumper. Leo is a horse of few words that mostly begin with the letter 'W'.
Who, What, Where, Why?

THE INTERVIEW

It had been a lazy Sunday for the horses. The jumping boys had been out in the paddock, and dinner had just been served. The girls and boys were quietly munching on their hay, but Nosey was bored, even though eating was his favourite pastime. Well, joint favourite. His other favourite was talking, and the time for that was right now!

'I've got an idea,' said Nosey. 'Like we see on TV sometimes. Well, I'm going to interview each of you. What do you think?'

'What?' said Leo.

Nosey continued, 'Well, you know, I ask you questions and you answer.'

'When?' said Leo again.

'When I ask the question, silly! Right, who wants to go first?' asked Nosey.

'Yeah, I'll go first,' replied Rumbo.

'OK. This is Nosey reporting for the stables documentary. Welcome, and what's your name?'

'You know my name!' said Rumbo.

'Yeah, I know your name, but this is all part of the interview, so you answer the questions, big bum!'

'Alright. Hello, Nosey, I'm Rumbo.'

'Excellent, and how old are you and what colour are you?' asked Nosey.

'Well, I'm three years old and I'm black,' said Rumbo.

'Right,' said Nosey, 'and have you always been that colour?'

'Well, yeah, I think so. Occasionally when I lay down, I sometimes get a bit of poo on my neck, and that's a different colour,' Rumbo replied.

'Alright, too much detail there. That's disgusting. But let's talk a bit more about that. Do you lay in poo regularly?'

'Well…' said Rumbo, 'I don't do it on purpose, but in the night, when it's dark, I can't see where it is, and then in the morning I get brushed, so it doesn't matter.'

'Very good,' said Nosey. 'And what line of work are you in?'

'Errr,' said Rumbo. 'I'm into dressage, but I've only just started. I do a lot of circles and straight lines and a lot of trotting, it seems. I sometimes get tired, and so then I stop and I get washed, and then I come home and sleep and eat, or eat then sleep.'

'Excellent. Well, thanks for that, Rumbo. I'll come back to you later. Now, Flo, would you like to tell me your name, please, and what colour you are?'

'Thank you. Um, my name is Flo. My whole name is Flo Jo, but most people call me Flo. Or Princess Flo. You can call me Flo. Did I mention my mother was a princess? Her name was April, and she was very famous, and they all called her a princess, and that means that I'm probably a princess, and my mother was brown, and I'm brown too.

'Most princesses are brown, that's what my mother used to say, and she also said that I was a princess and I have pretty feet and a pretty face, but that's because I'm a princess and...'

'Yeah, alright then. Next question,' interrupted Nosey. 'What work do you do on a regular basis?'

'Well, I'm a dressage princess, like my mother, 'cause she was a Grand Prix dressage princess. I go to the school, and I point my toes, and a lot of people watch me because I'm a princess and 'cause they knew my mother, and often they *oooh* and *aahhh* over me 'cause that's what they do when they see a princess.'

'Right, that's enough about you, Flo,' said Nosey.

'I can't hear it any more, so we will come back to you shortly, perhaps if we run out of conversation!'

'Now, Coco, could you give me a run down on who you are and what colour you are and what you do?'

'My name is Coco, and I'm dark brown, and I'm a Grand Prix dressage lady.'

Nosey interrupted, 'Ah, you're a lady, are you? That's very interesting, carry on.'

'Yes, I'm a lady, or mare, as they call it, and I train very hard every day and have been training for many years, and I'm generally quite shy, but I do love the excitement of the horse shows. I do love getting my mane all plaited up and looking all beautiful, and I have won many rosettes, and I have had my picture taken and...'

'Alright, well, we don't want to go on and on and on about your success, Coco. We all know that you are the cleverest, but, you know, we need to give everyone else a say as well.

'So, Charmeur, it's your turn now. Tell us what's it like not having a colour and what you do each day.'

Charmeur answered, 'My name is Charmeur, I'm sixteen years old and I do have a colour. I'm white, but the technical term is grey.'

'Well, that's debatable, isn't it?' interrupted Nosey.

' 'Cause to me it doesn't look like you or Leo have a colour, and *everyone* has a colour, so how do you explain that then?'

'I do have a colour and so does Leo. We are both grey, and my parents were grey, and their parents were grey and so on and so forth.'

'So, basically you come from a generation of horses that don't have a colour. Well, that's a shame. Does it make you jump any better, or do you think it helps that a lot of people can't see you?'

'Everyone can see me, and I don't know if it makes me jump better, but I am a Grand Prix show jumper, and I have won rosettes for jumping and had my photo taken lots of times, and I don't want to carry on this interview any more 'cause it's ridiculous,' said Charmeur.

'Very well,' said Nosey. 'So you've got nothing more to say then?'

'Only that I live next door to Leo and he smells!' Charmeur said, chuckling.

'So, Leo,' Nosey said, 'what have you got to say about that then, stinky?'

'What?' said Leo.

Nosey continued, 'You know, the fact that you smell a lot.'

'When?' said Leo.

'Well, I don't know, but Charmeur does complain about it a lot. So, Leo, tell us then about your show jumping and exactly what you think about when you go into the arena.'

'Eerrr, what?' said Leo.

Nosey rolled his eyes and said, 'You know, like you get all dressed up, and you're taken into the riding hall, and you jump around a lot, and then you come back home, and you go out in the field, and you don't really do a lot there, and you go to shows, and then you always seem to come back!'

'When?' said Leo.

'Oh, for goodness sake, Leo. You're spoiling the interview,' said Nosey.

'Cor, you're useless, you stinky pants!' said Charmeur.

Leo wasn't bothered. He was too busy munching on his hay. He was so laid back. He was just one of those horses who never seemed to be bothered. He got his work done and was a horse of few words!

'Right,' said Nosey, 'Charmeur, you interview me now, and don't ask anything complicated, OK, just the standard interviewing questions that will make me look good!'

'OK,' said Charmeur. 'So, Nosey, tell us about yourself.'

Nosey took a deep breath. 'Right, well, good evening, everyone. My name is Nosey, and I'm a chestnut horse, and I'm very tall and strong, and I do dressage. I'm very good at counting and balancing, and

I'm six years old, and I occasionally get bored when I go to school, and I'm sometimes quite naughty, and

then I do a big buck and then I get told off but I don't care, 'cause then I'm naughty again, and I live next door to Rumbo. I tell him what to do, and sometimes I go into the paddock and I eat a lot of grass, and I also like to sing, but I don't know all the words, so I just make them up! And I always have my head over the door so I always know what's going on, and I know probably the most gossip, and I eat a lot of hay. Right, now I'm gonna ask you all a question. We all have to tell a secret that we have never told anyone before. So, Rumbo, tell me something that you did that no one else knows about!'

Rumbo paused for a moment. He was thinking long and hard. Everyone was looking up at him, eager to know what his big secret was, but all he could manage was to mumble. 'I blah, blah, blah, blah, blah, stable!'

'What did you just say?' asked Nosey 'Speak up,

Rumbo. We didn't hear you!'

'I pooed in your stable once, through the bars!' said Rumbo, looking most guilty.

'Well, that's disgusting, and I can't believe I didn't notice. When did you do that?' said Nosey.

'While you were out being ridden,' said Rumbo.

'Right then, now it's my turn,' said Nosey. 'Well, Rumbo, once they forgot to close my door, and while you were out in the field, I went in and ate all your hay, so there. Right, well, I don't want to talk about it anymore. Just the thought of what you

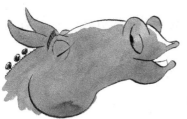 did makes me sick. I hope I can sleep, let alone still count tomorrow. Listen up, big bum, just watch what you're doing from now on,

19

and don't do it again, 'cause it's disgusting, got it?'

'Well,' said Rumbo. 'you did ask, and I told you the truth because it was an interview, and besides, you ate all my hay.'

'Well, count yourself lucky I don't eat all your hay tonight. Now I'm not talking any more. I got a lot of thinking to do!' And with that, Nosey turned his back on Rumbo.

Everyone else stayed quiet. Sometimes the truth hurts, but even though both boys were in the wrong, it wouldn't change the fact they were neighbours and still friends. And besides, their conversation certainly made for excellent entertainment for everyone else who stayed quiet!

THE FIELD

The sun was shining. It was a beautiful summer's day and being a Sunday, the only day off for everyone; it was the perfect day to go out and have fun in the field. Sure enough, the grooms came in, headcollars in hand.

'Yeah, we are going out today!' said Nosey. 'I told you, Rumbo. And I know I'm gonna be put in the biggest field 'cause I'm almost the biggest and I eat a lot, and, errr, well, 'cause I'm quite…'

Charmeur interrupted, 'Look, Nosey, it doesn't matter which field we go in. The grass is the same colour and it all tastes the same.'

'Well,' said Nosey. 'That's not true, 'cause when you and Leo have been in the field, it smells much worse. Leo rolls all over the place and you eat all the grass. Sometimes there are others who might want a little bit of grass. You should consider sharing!'

'Sharing?' said Charmeur. 'You don't know what sharing is. I've never seen you share any of your food!'

Nosey interrupted, 'Well, of course not. I'm hungry, aren't I, and I gotta concentrate lots *and* I'm growing!'

'Growing?' said Charmeur. 'The only thing that is growing is your belly!'

'I'm growing lots!' Rumbo said. 'I've grown out of all my rugs, and I heard my mum say that she hopes I don't grow any more. She said I was almost as big as her house, and that's *really* big!'

It was time. Charmeur and Leo were led out of the stable, and Nosey and Flo followed in close pursuit. Leo was so slow, the groom was practically dragging him along.

Flo was getting most annoyed with Leo's lazy amble towards the field. She couldn't help but say, 'Will you hurry up, Leo, you're holding us all up. "A moment's hesitation is wasting time," my mother, who was a princess, used to say. "Don't waste time, don't dawdle, make the most of everyday".'

Nosey interrupted, 'Your mother used to say a lot, didn't she?

It sounds like no one else got a word in when she was around. I think Leo is doing it on purpose. For goodness sake the smell coming off him lingers in the air when he walks slower. I think I'm gonna have to complain to somebody about it when I get back.

Flo, remind me to discuss this matter at dinner time, or after dinner, or at some point in the evening or sometime this week, if I have time. I'll have to check my schedule 'cause, with all these circles and shoulder-in practice with the counting stuff, I'm pretty chocka-block at the moment.'

Leo and Charmeur were led into the first field. It was a long narrow field next to an extremely large field full of prize-winning Aberdeen Angus cows, a big herd of thirty strong, brown, hairy cows!

To Flo's utter shock, her and Nosey were led into the field with the cows!

Flo said, 'I can't go in here, it's full of cows. I'm a princess. A princess! I don't mingle with this riff raff. I don't socialise with...'

Head collars were taken off and Nosey and Flo galloped as fast as possible to the tree at the end of the field.

Leo, on the other hand, had found a big piece of earth to roll in and was doing a very good job of getting as much dirt into his coat as possible. He rolled and rolled and rolled.

Charmeur thought rolling was a waste of time. He galloped as fast as he could and threw in a few giant bucks. He knew those Aberdeen Angus were watching, and although he was safe on the other side of the fence, he wanted to show them who was the biggest and strongest of them all. Leo had grown tired of rolling and had started eating the grass whilst lying down, but he soon got up and strolled over to the corner, which was half sheltered from the sun by the huge tree Nosey and Flo were taking refuge under. Charmeur joined the group, who by now were in deep discussion over the separating fence about the fact these cows were preventing Flo from grazing in the lush grass.

Flo pointed out, 'Look, I'm a princess – I'm not eating in the same field as those hairy monsters. I feel completely overwhelmed. Are even looking at me? Do they know who my mother is?'

'Who?' Asked Leo.

Flo continued, 'There, how can you not see them, Leo? They are everywhere. They are here and there, and they are eating all the grass, and they are looking at me, and they are eating with their mouths open, and, and, and, and…'

Charmeur interrupted 'Nosey, you should go and talk to them. Tell them who you are, and reason with them to share the field. Maybe then you will get an idea of what sharing is all about!'

Nosey said, 'Look, what are you trying to say? I know what sharing is. It's Flo that doesn't want to get involved with them. And besides, why do *I* have to go over?'

Charmeur replied, 'Well, Leo and I can't go over 'cause we are on the wrong side of the fence, and you are so good with words and so clever, Nosey. Explain to them that we are only out for a few hours – would they mind moving up the field a little so that we can have some grass?'

'That's a very good idea,' said Nosey, 'but keep an eye out. If they start closing in on me or looking angry, run around a lot and scare them away. I'll give you the signal of two loud snorts, and I'll bang my hoof on the floor like I've got an itch!'

Nosey started to walk very slowly towards the group of cows and then quickly turned around and came back to the tree.

'What are you doing?' said Charmeur.

Nosey replied, 'Well, I was just thinking – why doesn't Flo go over and talk to them. It's her that doesn't want to just stand by the fence, and to be perfectly honest, I'm not even hungry anymore. I had a big breakfast.'

Flo looked horrified. 'Nosey, I'm a princess. You should be honoured to go over. I can't go. I can't be seen talking to them. I can't go over there. You are big, you are tall, you can tell them who I am, that I'm a princess, and who my mother was, that she was a princess. I'm not going. I haven't been groomed yet and I can't go. I don't have…'

Nosey interrupted, 'Alright, alright, I'll go but I just

wanna say…'

'Say it when you come back!' interrupted Charmeur. Nosey turned around and started walking again towards the herd. He put his tail in the air. He thought that would impress them!

Nosey spotted a slightly smaller cow grazing on her own in the front. She had spotted him coming over, so he decided it was best to head straight for her. She was chewing on a big piece of grass. He didn't hesitate, he came straight out with it…

'Hello, I'm so sorry to interrupt you today. My name is Nosey.'

The pretty cow looked at Nosey and stopped chewing for a moment, obviously deep in thought. Then she just carried on chewing! Nosey was looking into her big brown eyes, she was looking back at him, and he couldn't help but think to himself that she was actually really pretty. He almost felt his heart skip a beat.

He asked her, 'What's your name?'

The cow stopped chewing again.

Nosey was captivated by her big brown eyes blinking at him.

Then she started chewing again.

Nosey continued, 'Look, don't be shy. You can tell me your name. I'm not gonna tell anyone, except maybe all my friends over there under the tree and my friends in the stables too…'

Nosey looked at everyone under the tree. They were

all staring back at him completely motionless, like statues. Then the cow let out the most enormous, deafening, *Moooooo!* and Nosey jumped out of his skin.

'Cor, you don't have to shout so loud! Right, well, now we have got that out of the way, Mrs Moooooo, once again my name is Nosey, and I live across the road there in the stables, and basically I'm a dressage horse, and, errr, I do dressage very well, and I count a lot, and I can count up to, ummm, three or four, which I'm willing to show you…'.

Back at the tree the group waited patiently… and waited… and waited… it seemed like forever! All they could see was the cow chewing grass and Nosey's lower jaw working overtime jabbering away. Charmeur said, 'Cor, she must be very difficult to reason with.

He hasn't stopped talking!'

Flo said, 'Well, there's an awful lot to tell her about me and my mother and my routine and my...'

'Who?' said Leo.

'The cow,' said Flo.

'Where?' said Leo.

'The cow that Nosey's talking to. He's been gone ages. I've lost count how many times I've swished my tail. It's gonna be time to go in soon!' said Flo.

As soon as she had closed her mouth, the group spotted the grooms approaching the fence with lead ropes in hand!

Charmeur said, 'Come on, we are out of here. Hurry, hurry, lets go! 'Nosey heard the thunder of hoof prints and realised it was home time. He said, 'Well, Mrs Moooo, it's been a delight talking to you, but I really have to go now, and I do hope to meet you again, very soon, and tell you the rest of everything that I'd like to tell you.' And with that, Nosey dashed for the fence.

Back at the yard questions were flying. Everyone wanted to know what the cow had to say and what had been the outcome of the two hour conversation that Nosey had all by himself.

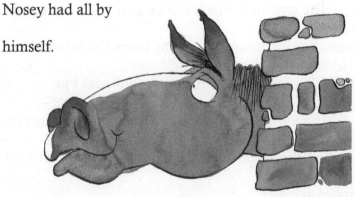

'Well,' said Nosey, 'to tell you the truth, I never actually got around to discussing the grazing issue, because by the time I had finished telling her about my dressage, and about my breakfast, and about my circles, and about my counting... well, then the time was gone.

I was just about to talk about the field thing when we had to come in, but she was a reasonable lady and, I must say, very pretty, and I don't think it would be a problem to share the field, and to be honest, I'm quite tired, 'cause it was a lot of concentrating I had to do, and I'm gonna have my lunch now, so we can talk more about it later...'

Everyone was looking on in total shock. They couldn't believe that Nosey hadn't asked the cow to move up the field. The bickering and conversation flew around the stables. But Nosey was silent, eating his hay. Looking out of the window, he was quietly remembering his wonderful conversation with Mrs Moooo. He thought about her beautiful eyes, her perfectly sized ears, her gleaming coat, and sighed to himself. This really could be it, this really might be how it feels... it just might be... Nosey had fallen in love!

THE BIG JUMP

osey was tacked up and ready to go into the riding school for his lessons of the day. Rumbo popped his head over the door and said, 'You going to school now, Nosey?'

Nosey started laughing.

'What's so funny?' said Rumbo.

'Nothing important,' said Nosey, chuckling to himself.

'Well, if you've got something to say, you might as well share it with everyone,' said Rumbo.

Nosey looked over again. 'Well, Rumbo, you've

got a space in your mouth! It looks really funny. But I wouldn't smile if I were you!'

Rumbo had noticed a strange sensation but hadn't realised that one of his front baby teeth had fallen out!

'Yeah, I think you've lost a tooth or something,' said Nosey.

Rumbo looked down on the yard floor, and sure enough, there was a baby tooth lying on the floor.

'Oh yes, there's my tooth. Well, what shall I do? I can't reach it all the way down there.'

Nosey laughed again. 'Yeah, it's a goner, that one. Shame that.'

'What do you mean?' asked Rumbo.

Nosey said, 'Well, the first time I lost a tooth I

found it in my manger, so I put it under the hay before I went to sleep, and then the next morning the tooth fairy must have taken it, 'cause I couldn't find it anywhere. And when my mummy came in, she had a new blanket for me, so you see, the tooth fairy must have sold it and got me a blanket instead. It was a big one as well, 'cause it was really cold at the time.'

Rumbo looked excited. A brand new blanket! He had given his blanket a good chew over the past few weeks, which may have been the reason for the wobbly tooth.

But just as Nosey left to go to school, the grooms came in to sweep the floor and swept Rumbo's tooth right away! It was gone in a flash! Rumbo didn't know what to say, but Flo tried to comfort him. 'Well, my mother said you shouldn't believe in tooth fairies, and it's gone now, Rumbo, too late, too slow, fuss over

nothing…' her voice faded into the background as poor

Rumbo went back into his stables to munch his hay.

He secretly contemplated how lovely it would have

been to have a new blanket. But he had lots more teeth

in his mouth, and if chewing on his blanket had made

his teeth wobbly, well, think how many blankets he

could get with the rest of his teeth. He snickered to himself. There was no time like the present, no time to waste. It was time to chew. Those teeth would be coming out in no time if he had anything to do with it!

Meanwhile, Nosey was warming up in the riding hall. Dressage was a very detailed, sophisticated job, and although he enjoyed performing, Nosey found the whole counting rhythm and concentration thing rather boring.

For him, a little naughtiness was sometimes the

only way to have fun at school, and today was going to be one of those days. The jumps had been set up, and he knew Charmeur would be in soon. He already had a few plans up his sleeve. But today, unusually, he was being ridden towards some jumping poles lain on the ground. Nothing he couldn't manage though. Just got to walk over them, that's all. Simple!

Bang! Whoops! Nosey said, 'Tripped over that one.' *Bang! Clonk!* 'Whoops a daisy.' Nosey just couldn't seem to step over the poles. His big feet kept hitting them!

Chameur came in, looking very smart, all booted up and ready for his jumping training. Nosey again walked over the set of poles.

Bang! Clonk! Bang! Clonk!

He managed to step on every pole. 'Whoops! Whoops a daisy! Whoops!'

Nosey caught a glimpse of Charmeur looking most amused at his clumsiness.

'Who put those there?' Nosey said loudly. 'I could have broken my leg on that! That's really dangerous, that is. I could have been injured. I could have died! My whole life flashed before my eyes. I'm gonna have to report that to someone.'

Charmeur rolled his eyes.

'Well, if you looked where you were going, you would have seen the poles on the floor. I saw them as soon as I came into the riding hall.'

Nosey answered, 'I *was* looking where I was going, silly. I've got my eyes open, you know!'

'Clearly not,' Charmeur interrupted. 'You obviously can't see past the end of your nose!'

'What you trying to say about my nose?' said Nosey.

'Well,' said Charmeur 'It's a bit big, your nose, isn't

it?'

'I can't see it looks that big. Anyway, you're just jealous – at least I've got a colour!' Nosey giggled.

'I do have a colour, you wally. I'm grey,' said Charmeur.

'No,' said Nosey, 'you've been washed too much. They've washed your colour right off. You look naked! I bet your owner can't even find you when it snows!'

Charmeur was furious. He didn't want to have this discussion before he jumped. It took a lot of power to clear those big fences, and wasting energy on a naughty Nosey was pointless. He turned to Nosey and said, 'Oh, you dressage horses are so snooty and posh, you need to keep your feet on the ground and come back down to earth.'

Nosey said, 'That's really funny coming from someone who doesn't have a colour!'

Charmeur came straight back, 'Well, Leo and I think dressage is a girls sport!'

'Oh, be quiet,' replied Nosey. 'Don't you think everyone stares up your bum when you jump over a fence! Anyway, I'm not talking to you anymore. You haven't got a colour.'

'Big Nose!'

'Snowflake!'

'Clumsy!'

The remarks kept exchanging, but it didn't stop either from warming up. It was time to do some work!

The jumps got bigger and bigger and Charmeur was on top form.

He hadn't knocked a single fence down. He was very pleased with himself. He had been concentrating really hard and blocking out Nosey's dressage movements, even though they sometimes crossed right in front of him. When the final combination was set up, Charmeur's heart was beating so fast that the sweat was built up on his neck. This was the final jump of the day in preparation for his big competition on the weekend.

Nosey was working around the edge of the school. He knew dressage was all about rhythm and balance, and he was always talking to himself, keeping count as he went round.

Just as Charmeur was put into a canter and brought around for the approach to the combination fences, Nosey said in a very loud voice, 'One, two, three, four, one, three, two, four, two, four, three, three…'

Charmeur was so busy listening to this incorrect counting that he totally miscounted his own approach and knocked down the fence.

He was furious!

'Nosey, I can't concentrate when you're counting out loud, and you're not even counting correctly!' he shouted.

Nosey looked up and said, 'Well, I can't concentrate when you keep leaping off the ground and breathing so loud.'

'Look, I have to jump again now. Can you keep it down a bit?'

'Well,' said Nosey, 'I'll try, but I'll tell you what…' It was too late. Charmeur was already in approach and before Nosey could say another thing had soared over both fences at such height that even Nosey was impressed by his agility and power. Charmeur was very proud of himself and was well rewarded with a polo mint and a big pat on the neck by his rider.

Nosey walked past and said, 'Look, Snowflake, let's make a deal, alright. When we go back to the stables, you won't tell anyone that I counted wrongly, and I won't tell anyone that you knocked a fence down and that everyone was staring up your bum. Do we have a deal?' Charmeur thought for a moment. Being a bit older and wiser, he knew that this was secretly Nosey's way of apologising, so he looked at Nosey and said, 'Nosey, your secret is safe with me. That's why we're friends. But, listen, don't make any snowflake comments in the stables. I've got a reputation, you know!'

Nosey looked pleased and said, 'Yeah, alright then, it's a deal.' Both boys went back home, tired and confident, knowing their friendship was intact.

Some horses are bred to jump, whilst others are bred to dance. Both have talent, and both work hard, but in different disciplines.

They were different colours, different breeding, different ages, but both beautiful in their own way.

DINNER TIME

It was nearly dinner time in the yard. Meal times were always a highlight. You could hear the boys and girls stomachs rumbling in anticipation...

'Yum, yum, yum,' Rumbo said. 'Yum, yum, yum, I can feel it in my tum. Hey, that rhymes, that does!'

'Yeah,' said Nosey. 'So does "Yum, yum, yum, you gotta big bum! That's really funny that is – you gotta really big bum!'

'That's not very nice,' Rumbo said.

'I can't believe your language, Nosey,' blurted Flo. 'If my mother was here, she would have told you off.

She was a princess, you know. It's not correct to use such rude words – you should say bottom or rear end. My mother was classically trained. She would be furious if she heard you speak like that. I don't know; just the thought of it makes me... makes me... makes me... well, I don't know. I don't even want to think of it. It's disgusting, despicable. Uh, I'm disgraced to be involved in this. I'm a princess. I shouldn't have to listen to these rude words!'

'Well,' said Nosey, 'nothing rhymes with bottom, so I can't use that word, can I?'

Rumbo's eyes suddenly open wide. 'Dinner's here!'

The scoops of food were dropped into the mangers. You could hear the chomping and chewing.

Chomp, chomp, chomp!

'I love my dinner, I do,' said Rumbo, his head out of the door to check no one got more than him. The only problem was that Rumbo had a tendency to talk with his mouth full, a tendency that the birds had picked up on. A free meal was a free meal, and they all knew Rumbo always had something to say while he was eating.

The little birds flew down to pick up the oats and country mix on the floor right outside

his door. 'Oi, that's my dinner!' Rumbo protested.

'Stop,' *chomp* eating...'

'My...' *chomp, chomp, chomp* '...food!'

Flo came out to see what all the noise was about. 'Well, you shouldn't eat with your mouth open. My mother always said a lady never eats with her mouth open. My mother was a princess, you know, and that makes me a princess!'

'You should mind your own business. They're eating my dinner,' said Rumbo, as another mouthful of mix dropped on the floor.

Nosey looked out. 'Yeah, they're eating all your food, you silly billy. They're not getting any of mine. I don't share anything.'

'Well, that's hardly anything to be proud of,' said Flo. 'My mother was a princess. She was most generous. She always said share and share a like. My mother was always kind and generous. She was a princess, you know.'

'We all know that,' said Nosey. 'You tell us that a hundred times a day. To be honest with you, I'm getting sick of hearing it. You know, you're putting me off my food!'

Suddenly the stable banter was brought to a halt as Andrew walked in with his new mobile. A distinct clicking noise was to be heard coming from it.

'Come on, Leo,' Andrew said, 'put your head out of the door. Let me take a picture of you. Come on, Leo, smile, good boy.' **_Click!_**

'That's it!' said Andrew, 'and again, good boy.'

'Who?' said Leo.

'Oi, dippy!' said Charmeur. 'He wants you to smile!'

'But I've got food in my teeth!' said Leo, as the camera went *Click! Click! Click!*

'Well,' said Charmeur, 'that's hardly the biggest problem you've got!'

'What's that supposed to mean?' said Leo.

'You smell, don't you!' blurted Charmeur.

'I don't smell!' said Leo, very upset by the comment.

Click! Click! Click!

'Cor,' he continued, 'I wasn't even looking straight that time. Stop disturbing me, Charmeur. Anyway, you can't smell on a picture, you wally!'

Charmeur immediately corrected him. 'Of course you can.' With a very serious voice, he went, 'It's the technology these days.'

'What do you mean?' said Leo.

Charmeur continued, 'It's these smell phones, isn't it!'

Sadly Leo had been away the time the Americans had ambled through the yard talking about their cell phones, and unfortunately Charmeur's hearing wasn't quite what it used to be. His hairy ears didn't help much!

'Well, I don't know,' Leo said. 'If I look so bad, why is he taking my picture then and not yours?'

'He's not trying to sell me, is he!' said Charmeur.

Leo answered, very upset, 'Well, that's not nice. I'm jumping well, doing my best.'

'Am I bothered?' Charmeur interrupted. 'Do I look bothered? Talk to the hoof 'cause the face ain't listening!'

'Well, that's charming,' Leo said.

'Ah, be quiet, stinky pants,' said Chameur.

A quiet cackle was heard from Nosey's corner.

Dinner and hay was finally through, and with the boys' and girls' stomachs finally filled, the lights were turned out and another busy day was slowly coming to an end. All the horses were tired, especially poor Rumbo. He had had his first day at school that day, and at three years old, he was the youngest in the yard, not to mention one of the biggest. So he lay down, shut his eyes and quietly drifted off to sleep, dreaming of all those things he had thought of during the day, and no doubt imagining how hungry he would be at breakfast time!

All of a sudden, someone let out an enormous snore!

Nosey said, 'What the hell was that?'

And again this rumbling snore came out of the dark!

'Right, that's it,' said Nosey. 'I can't sleep with that noise. I can't even think, it's so loud. I can't get any peace and quiet here. How am I supposed to think? How am I supposed to sleep? It's coming from Rumbo. He's a snorer. You gotta watch those snorers. They're always causing trouble, especially in the dark!'

Everyone else was asleep. Nosey was the last one awake – he would have to be the one to wake a sleeping Rumbo.

'Rumbo, Rumbo…. *Ruuummmbo!*' shouted Nosey.
But there was no response. The snores just continued.
Even worse, they seemed to be getting louder!

Nosey decided the only thing left to do was to kick
the adjoining wall.

The shock of that should wake Rumbo quickly enough!

Sure enough, after one sharp kick, Rumbo lifted his
head in shock. Nosey could see the whites of his eyes
in the darkness.

'What's going on?' said Rumbo, still half asleep.

'I'm tryin' to get to sleep… but someone is snoring!' Nosey said in a furious tone.

'What are you waking me up for then?' said Rumbo, looking most confused.

Nosey replied, 'Because, big bum, it's you that is snoring, isn't it!'

'I didn't hear anything!' proclaimed Rumbo. 'I was asleep!'

Nosey didn't hesitate in announcing, 'I'm telling you, you were snoring, that's a fact, and I'm sick of it. You snore really loud. I can't sleep, I can't think – I can't even think about sleeping! I get no peace, no quiet. It's ridiculous!'

'Well,' said Rumbo, 'How do you know it was coming from me?'

' 'Cause,' said Nosey, 'I live next door to you. The noise was definitely coming from you! In fact, I'm gonna call you Rumble from now on, 'cause the whole ground was rumbling when you snored. You might have caused an earthquake!'

'I didn't know you can cause an earthquake from snoring,' said Rumbo.

'Well, it could be possible' said Nosey. 'We will ask Flo in the morning. Chances are she will know, and if she doesn't know, she might know someone who does… and if she doesn't, then we will ask Coco, 'cause she knows everything. She's Grand Prix, you know. She's really clever.'

'Well, OK,' Rumbo said. 'I don't know, but can I go back to sleep now 'cause I'm really tired?'

'Yeah, go on then, but, Rumble, if you snore again, there will be trouble. I'm watching you, Rumble pants!'

Rumbo laid back down. There was no point arguing now. Some fights were simply not worth having, and besides, breakfast would be coming soon, and that was far more exciting than having a midnight discussion with Nosey… or Noisy as Rumbo secretly liked to call him!

THE COMPETITION

Sunday morning was usually the horses' day off, but today there was a distinct excitement in the air. It was competition time!

Nosey had been training hard for this day. Coco, being a very experienced Grand Prix horse, didn't need to practise the test, but Nosey had never been to a show before, and his rider had been going through the test and movements all week long. Nosey was quite confident he knew his test off by heart.

Coco was brought out of her stable, and the preparation began of getting her plaited up and groomed.

'I think it's ridiculous that we have to get up so early,' said Nosey. 'It's Sunday, after all. We don't normally have to get up this early!'

Flo was quick to point out, 'I don't know why you're complaining, Nosey. We've all been woken up and we don't even have to go to the competition. My mother used to go to many competitions and get up early all the time, and my mother…'

Nosey interrupted, 'I don't care what your mother had to say. It sounds like she never stopped talking, and to be perfectly honest, it's too early to even have a discussion about anything right now. I'm just happy I don't have to have my hair plaited like Coco, 'cause it's obviously a girl thing, 'cause it only happens to girls when they go to a competition.'

With this, Nosey was led out of the stable, and to

his utter horror the groom started to plait his mane!

Rumbo looked over his door and couldn't help but say, 'Oh, Nosey, that's really funny, cause now you're having your mane plaited, and didn't you just say that that it's a girl thing?' Nosey was quite embarrassed and snapped back, 'I said, Rumbo, it's a great thing and only happens to great horses when they go to a competition. You should listen better when I'm talking, Rumbo. You obviously have hay in your ears or something. Yeah, hay in your ears, and that's why you can't hear me properly!'

Rumbo shook his head and said, 'Hey, I don't think

I have hay in my ears. I think I'd notice if I had hay in my ears. Hey, Charmeur, do I look like I have hay in my ears? Can you see any hay? Hey... hey!?'

Charmeur wasn't getting involved. He kept his head down and carried on eating his breakfast, which only made Nosey feel hungrier. His belly started to rumble louder and louder!

As Nosey's class was early on and Coco's later in the day, Nosey was loaded first into the trailer and transported to the show ground, which was buzzing with excitement. Flags were flying and flapping in the wind and a loud speaker was playing music. Lots of horses were warming up for the classes, and the ring organiser was calling out the horses next into the arena and the results at the end of each test. Nosey could hardly contain himself. He was finding it hard to keep still and was trying to concentrate on remembering his test, which he had been practising all week. The trailers were parked close to each other, and he could hear the other horse next door quietly munching on hay, waiting to be brought out.

Nosey started reciting his test out loud, and as his side door was open, he could see the horse next door was watching his every move.

'Right, I've gotta go up the centre line, and then halt for a bit and stand still while my rider salutes the judge, and then I start to trot again, and then I turn left, and then I go across the school and I do a faster trot, and then I do a circle, which I'm very good at 'cause I like circles, and I'll make sure I do that circle well, and I might just put my tail up a bit, so it looks like I'm concentrating on my circle, and then I, I, I ummm...'

The horse next door was listening to Nosey's every word. Nosey looked over at him and said a big, 'Hello,

I'm Nosey, what's your name then?'

The horse paused for a moment before answering him in a very strong German accent.

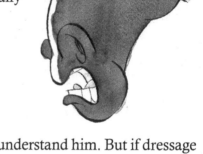

'Good day to you, Mr Sir. My name is Heindrick, and I originally come from Hamburg. Have you been to this competition before?'

Nosey could hardly understand him. But if dressage were a talking competition, Nosey would easily win!

'Well, it's a pleasure to meet you, Hindleg. No, I haven't been to any competitions before. This is my first one, but I have been training for quite a few years now, and I have been practising my counting and circles a lot. In fact, I can count very well, and I do love counting and circles. I'm very good at circles, in fact.

I do a circle every day, probably several times a day. I've lost count of how many circles I've done, 'cause when I start counting Charmeur or Flo distract me. But you don't know them, so there's no point in me talking about that. It's very interesting that you come from Hamburger. It sounds like a very interesting place, but I can't talk now, as much as I would like to talk to you, 'cause I have to concentrate on my test, and I can see my rider is coming now. She had to go and tell them that I am here, 'cause they have probably been waiting for me, 'cause, you know, I'm going to be famous one day. Did you know that, Hindleg?'

'My name is Heindrick, not Hindleg,' Heindrick pointed out.

Before he could reply, Nosey was taken out of the trailer. He could hardly stand still long enough for his rider to get on. He was suddenly overcome with excitement. He trotted over to the warming up area, which was full of horses trotting and cantering around. Nosey didn't know where to look first. He couldn't contain himself and started jumping around. The more he jumped, the more the other horses seemed to get excited too. Nosey was so excited that his jumps turned into bucks and leaps, and he caused total chaos in the arena. He bucked so much that his rider fell off!

Nosey was so busy, with his head between his front legs and his back legs in the air, that he never even noticed, and it was only after several laps of galloping around and disturbing the entire arena full of horses that he slowed down and noticed that he was now riderless.

'Well, this is ridiculous!' said Nosey. 'How on earth am I meant to carry on without my rider, I tell you? I just have a couple of minutes of warming up, and my rider decides to go and leave me. I better go back to the trailer. She's probably waiting for me there or something.'

Nosey quickly cantered over to his trailer, where Heindrick was still munching his hay next door.

'What are you doing back here so quickly? Heindrick said. 'You only left about ten minutes ago. Where is your rider? You left here with your rider, and now you return without her. This is very strange behaviour!'

Nosey, breathing heavily from his galloping around, answered, 'Well, Haynet, I went over to the warming up arena, where there were lots of other horses, and then the music was playing and all the people were there to watch me, so I got excited and I started to jump around. Then everyone started making a lot of noise, 'cause they were impressed with my jumping around, so I thought I would jump around a bit more, but then the other horses started jumping around as well, so I started jumping around like I was *really* jumping around, and then obviously my rider got so excited she jumped off! I carried on for a bit, but then I noticed my rider was missing. To be perfectly honest with you, I'm quite surprised that my rider couldn't control her excitement. She's left me to do the test alone, which, of course, is understandable, 'cause she knows I'm very good at counting and circles.'

As Nosey was talking, he suddenly thought he heard his name announced over the loud speaker. He had done. It was the announcer warning the other riders that there was a loose horse galloping around!

Nosey looked at Heindrick. 'I gotta go, Hoofpick. They just called me into the arena, but if my rider comes back looking for me, tell her I've gone to do the test and I'm very disappointed in the lack of support I've had on my first show. See you soon, Haynet.'

'My name is...' Heindrick tried to say.

'Not now, later...' interrupted Nosey, and he was off. He headed straight for the test arena, and failing to even notice the other horse in the middle of the test, trotted up the centre line and halted. There seemed to be an instant of total silence as everyone stood in utter shock at the situation in hand. Nosey suddenly had brain freeze.

He couldn't remember what he had to do next. He just stood like a statue. There was nothing left to do but run and run fast back to the trailer.

Heindrick was stunned to see Nosey back again. He had only just left!

'What is going on here? You only left a matter of moments ago, and it is clearly quite impossible that you managed to do the entire dressage test in this short amount of time, even if you were in a hurry and rushed around very fast, which is certainly not the dynamic approach that you should be taking towards this sport, which is designed to be elegant and composed!'

Nosey started rolling his eyes, 'Listen, Hairnet, I rushed over there and went up the centre line, and when I stopped to do that halting thing, I looked up and noticed that there was another horse already in the arena. I couldn't believe it – there's just a total lack of organisation here. I clearly heard my name announced, and what's more, when I went in I heard a few people shouting my name and pointing. So it was obviously my turn to go. Anyway, to be perfectly honest, when I saw the way the judges were looking at me, with big eyes, I lost my concentration. I couldn't remember what I had to do next.'

Heindrick interrupted him. 'Ah, Nosey, I do believe that your rider is coming over here now. You see her? She is being held up by those two rather handsome gentlemen. In fact, I do believe she is actually looking a little bit lame. Ah, yah, yes, very lame. It will be a miracle if she will be able to continue in such a state. What a terrible pity. I wonder what on earth happened to her. She does appear to have some serious grass stains on her jodhpurs.'

Nosey replied, 'I have to tell you, Hairnet, it's a

minefield out there. I just can't believe it really.

This day has gone from bad to worse. If it's not enough that I'm expected to go in and do the test alone, now my rider has gone lame! I better get her home as soon as possible. She will have to go to the clinic and there will probably be a vet waiting for her when we get home. It's just a disaster. Leave her for a few minutes and look what happens!'

Heindrick pointed out, 'From this angle, I can't be

exactly certain, but it seems to look like she has some rather large hoof prints on her bottom. It looks like a size six hind-leg shoe.'

Nosey looked horrified. That was exactly the size shoe he wore!

'Well, I think that's disgusting. I can't see why anyone would want to be walking around looking such a mess. I mean you can see the effort I made today. I got my hair plaited and everything. Look, Hindsight, it's been a pleasure meeting you, but I have to go see to my rider. Good luck today, and if anyone asks you where I've gone, just tell them I've gone home.'

On the trip home, Nosey thought hard about what he was going to say when he got back to the yard. No doubt he was going to be asked a lot of questions. The journey back seemed to fly by in a flash, and before long, he was being led back to the stable. He could hear Flo's voice before he even walked around the corner.

'He's here, he's here! Here he is. Well, Nosey, how was it? Did you win? Did you do well? Did you see anyone you know? Did you see anyone I know? Did anyone ask about me? Did they ask about my mother? Did they...'

Nosey interrupted, 'The entire show was cancelled due to the weather!'

Flo continued,

'What do you mean it was cancelled? It couldn't have been cancelled. The weather isn't bad. It hasn't been bad here. How bad was it?'

Nosey interrupted again, 'OK, OK, OK, it wasn't cancelled, but to tell you the truth, well, how am I going to put this? Do you want the good news or the bad news?'

Rumbo suddenly looked very interested. 'Let's hear the bad news!'

'Well,' said Nosey, 'the good news is that I turned up and I concentrated very well and I warmed up very quickly – much quicker than I had expected to, actually – and, everyone was extremely excited to see me. And then I went in, alone, I might add, to do my test, and the part of the test I did, I did extremely well... and then, well, then I left.'

There was a distinct silence in the yard.

'The bad news is that my rider decided to part company with me in the warm-up phase and only decided to return when I'd finished the test. And, I might add, somewhere along the line she somehow managed to go lame! So, Coco, you can take your plaits out, 'cause she won't be riding anyone for a few days. We will have to see what the vet says. To be perfectly honest with you, I think the entire showing experience is overrated, and if you have any further questions, I shall only be answering after my dinner, 'cause I'm very hungry now.'

Nosey went to the back of his stable and started munching on his hay. He was confident that he had tried his best. Every day is a new experience, and every experience is a lesson learned. And everyone knew that it's not always about winning but taking part and taking pride in what you do.

CHRISTMAS DAY

The snow was falling fast outside, and inside the stables it was cold, so cold that, as the horses drank, the water became icicles on their whiskers. But this didn't distract from the most important day in the calendar...

It was Christmas!

Christmas day was very important to the horses.

Take the year before for example. Their mum came in with loads of presents, blankets, head collars and lots of other useful things, but more importantly, everybody got the day off. No one had had to go to school, and all they did was eat, sleep, talk, eat, talk and sleep.

Nosey loved the Christmas songs. He made up his own words to the Christmas carols, not to everyone's taste, but he certainly gave everyone something to talk about!

They were all waiting with their heads over their doors. Charmeur and Leo already had their Christmas hats on, which the groom had brought in, and according to Rumbo's stomach, which was rumbling very loud, breakfast was on the way.

Nosey said, 'Rumbo, can you keep it down a bit. Your rumbling stomach is making such a racket. I can't concentrate. And I can see you breathing… You look like a dragon breathing smoke!'

'I can't help my tummy making noises,' said Rumbo. 'I'm hungry, and anyway, what are you concentrating on?'

'Well,' said Nosey,
'I'm concentrating
on what presents
I'm going to get
this year. Last year,
I concentrated all
morning and I didn't get anything I wanted, so this
year, I've been concentrating all night too, and we'll
see if it worked.'

'What?' said Leo.

'Oh, be quiet, stinky pants,' said Charmeur. 'I've
been trying to concentrate too, but your smell is
disturbing the atmospheric conditions of the weather.'

'What?' said Leo again.

'It's true,' said Charmeur. 'I heard it on the radio
weather forecast yesterday, so just be quiet, smelly.'

Flo looked absolutely horrified at Charmeur's statement.

'That is totally ludicrous,' she said. 'I'm a princess, and I've never heard anything so ridiculous! There is no possible way Leo's smell is affecting the weather. Good grief, if my mother were here, and you all know she was a princess, she would be horrified that such a conversation was being had on Christmas day. It's a special day, a nice day. Well, I, I just don't know what to say. I...'

'Breakfast is here!' interrupted Rumbo. 'Yum, yum, yum!'

After they finished their breakfast, Charmeur and Leo were put out in the paddock behind the stables. Nosey and Rumbo remained snug inside their box looking out over the field, which was deep with snow, but the jumping boys were a little older and needed to stretch their legs, even in the cold.

As Charmeur was led out, he said to Nosey, 'Look, keep me posted. Let me know if the presents come!'

'Over and out, snowflake,' said Nosey.

As he went round the corner, Charmeur gave Nosey a disapproving look.

The radio was on and the Christmas carols playing continuously. Suddenly 'Jingle Bells' came on, and

Nosey couldn't resist a sing along…

'Jingle bells, my rug smells, I eat the most hay, I can count to number ten, and my birthday is in May!'

Rumbo started laughing, and even Flo and Coco were smiling. This only encouraged Nosey, and he went into the second chorus in full swing…

'Jingle bells, Leo smells and I love my mum. When Charmeur jumps the jumps, I look up his bum!'

Well, Rumbo howled with laughter, Coco looked highly unimpressed and Flo was horrified.

'Yeah,' said Nosey, 'I like that one. It's my favourite. I've been thinking about it all day.' Coco was a lady of few words but she couldn't help but say in a quiet voice, 'Nosey, you shouldn't talk or sing about someone when they are not here. It's not fair and it's not right, OK?'

Nosey answered, 'Well, it's true, and besides, I can sing it again when they come in from the paddock if everyone wants me to!'

'No,' said Coco, 'that won't be necessary. We will keep this between us, but from now on, any singing will be with the right words only, please.'

'I don't know the right words,' said Rumbo. 'There's so many. I can hum though, if that's allowed?'

'Your stomach makes enough noise!' said Nosey. 'You don't need to hum along. It's hard enough to hear the radio when your stomach's talking anyway!'

Suddenly a voice came from outside. 'Are those presents there yet, Nosey?'

Nosey and Rumbo looked out of the window onto the paddock covered in snow.

It was hard enough making out the fencing, the snow was falling so rapidly. Nosey shouted out, 'Who said that, and who wants to know if the presents are here, and how do you know my name?'

The voice answered back, 'It's me, Charmeur, and Leo, you wally. Are they there yet or not?'

As hard as Rumbo and Nosey looked, they couldn't see Charmeur or Leo. They were so white they simply blended into the snow!

Nosey said, 'Look, I'm not telling anyone if the presents are here, especially when I can't see you!'

Charmeur was furious. He walked up to the fence and shouted back, 'Look, Nosey, stop messing around.

We are coming inside in a minute. Are the presents there or not?'

Rumbo could make out Charmeur's angry eyes looking right at him.

'It's Charmeur, all right! Those are his eyes.'

Nosey looked hard. 'Where's your body gone? I can only see your eyes.'

Charmeur was furious. Lucky for him and Leo, the grooms were coming to bring them in. And not a moment too soon – their whiskers were beginning to freeze!

Once the boys were back into their warm, straw-filled stables, their mum came around the corner with a big black sack!

Flo blurted out, 'Presents are here! I can feel I'm going to get something special, very special. My mother was a princess, you know, so I'm a princess too. It's

89

highly likely that I'm going to get something very special, 'cause princesses always do. I don't know what but something special, something… something sparkly, something wonderful… a tiara maybe, something for a princess.'

The bag was opened, and Coco was the first to be given a present.

She had been bought a shiny brass name plate for her door, and a new leather head collar also with a name plate on. This was very special. Only the competition horses had leather head collars and name plates.

Rumbo was next. He got a new blanket, blue in colour and very warm-looking. Rumbo was most pleased.

Then there was Leo and Charmeur. They were both bought new boots for jumping. They were made from leather, very smart, and would probably be saved for competitions.

Then it was Flo's turn. She got a new saddle cloth with her name embroidered on the side. It would certainly be a talking point in the riding hall.

Last but not least was Nosey.

The wait seemed like forever for Nosey. It had been agonising watching everyone get their presents before him. But then finally it was his turn, and he was shown his new bridle. It was a special one, with a diamanté brow band and shiny brown leather.

'Cor, look at that,' said Nosey.

'That's very nice. I really could do with a new bridle, and this one's all sparkly as well. They're probably going to be taking lots of photos of me in that, 'cause it looks really expensive, it does. It's like Coco's bridle, and she's really important, so that means I'm also really important, and that probably means I'm gonna have to count a lot more and concentrate harder too!'

Rumbo said, 'Yup, I wouldn't like to have

all that responsibility, so good luck with that, Nosey.'

'Well,' said Nosey, 'it comes with the job, 'cause the older you get the more you have to learn, the more you have to concentrate, and the more work you have to do. But the good thing is I'm probably gonna get more food now too, so that's good news, 'cause, I have to say, I have noticed I've been feeling a lot hungrier the last few weeks. I think it's all the concentrating and counting personally. I'm counting and concentrating on a regular basis, you know!'

Everyone looked around in amazement. No one else had noticed any difference in Nosey's concentrating or counting abilities, especially Charmeur, who knew exactly how good Nosey's counting was, and he knew, oh yes, he knew Nosey had a long way to go!

He couldn't help but comment. 'Well, Nosey,

counting is hardly one of your strong points, is it?'

'What are you trying to say?' said Nosey. 'Listen, Charmeur, you're lucky you both got presents, 'cause I think you shouldn't get presents if you haven't got a colour. Rumbo and I couldn't even see you when you were in the field. If Rumbo hadn't spotted your eyes, you might have been left outside – they might have thought you weren't there! You might have become a snowman, or a snow horse, in fact, 'cause I remember once someone who knew someone else said that a snowman was in the field, and it certainly wasn't there the day before, so obviously somebody must have been left outside overnight, and they turned into a snowman!'

'Cor, that must have hurt,' said Rumbo.

'Well,' said Nosey, 'I didn't see it myself, but I heard the rumour from someone that knew somebody else, so it's obviously true. Just count yourself lucky that we saw your eyes and that the grooms brought you inside in time, because you could have both turned into snowmen!'

'What?' said Leo.

'It was probably your smell that saved us,' Charmeur said to Leo. 'They probably followed the smell to track us down.'

'Who?' said Leo.

'Oh, be quiet, stinky!' said Charmeur.

It was a good Christmas, there was no doubt about it. Everyone was very pleased with their presents, and as they munched on their hay, and the snow fell outside, and Christmas carols played on the radio, the boys and girls relaxed and rested, thinking what a lovely day it had been so far and with lunch and dinner still to come.

It was time for reflection and thought, peace and quiet, and a feeling of love that filled the stables.

They were lucky to have each other.

Friendship is the best present of them all.